Millie and id

~ For Aaron ~

PUFFIN BOOKS

Published by the Penguin Group
Penguin Books Ltd, 27 Wrights Lane, London W8 5TZ, England
Penguin Books USA Inc., 375 Hudson Street, New York, New York 10014, USA
Penguin Books Australia Ltd, Ringwood, Victoria, Australia
Penguin Books Canada Ltd, 10 Alcorn Avenue, Toronto, Ontario, Canada M4V 3B2
Penguin Books (NZ) Ltd, 182–190 Wairau Road, Auckland 10, New Zealand

Penguin Books Ltd, Registered Offices: Harmondsworth, Middlesex, Engaland

First published by Hamish Hamilton Ltd 1996
Published in Puffin Books 1997
1 3 5 7 9 10 8 6 4 2

Made and printed in Italy by Printers srl – Trento

Millie and the Mermaid

Penny Ives

PUFFIN BOOKS

It was the very first day of Millie's very first visit to her great aunt Pearl.

Aunt Pearl was a
lighthouse keeper
who sent the bright
light out over the sea
every night.

"Yippee!" Millie shouted, opening the front door.
"It's a sunny day. Can we go to the beach, Auntie?"
"I think that's a lovely idea," said Aunt Pearl.

Millie had never seen the sea before. She gazed at all the people bobbing about in the water.

"Everyone can swim except for me," she said sadly.

"And me," laughed Aunt Pearl. "I've lived by the sea all my life but I've always been too busy to learn to swim. Why don't we make a sandcastle instead?"

So Millie made an enormous sandcastle, bigger than anyone else's. Then she dug a huge hole. But she still wanted to go swimming.

"Would you like to bury me in the sand, dear?" suggested Aunt Pearl generously.

"All right," said Millie.

But although she worked hard all afternoon until only Aunt Pearl's head was showing, it still wasn't swimming.

After tea Millie sat at the window, watching the waves and combing her tangled hair.

"Goodness, Millie," said Aunt Pearl. "You look just like a mermaid! All you need is a little fish's tail."

"And then perhaps I could swim," sighed Millie.

That night Millie
dreamed of the sea.
She saw mermaids draped in
seaweed and pearls from sunken
treasure. The mermaids combed
their hair and sang sweet songs
to pirate ships.

They slipped in and out between shoals of silver fish.

The next morning Millie couldn't stop thinking about the mermaids.

"I *must* learn to swim," she told Aunt Pearl.

"We'd better begin right away, then," said Aunt Pearl.
"But you'll need some help to keep you afloat."
On the way down to the beach she bought Millie a
pair of red water-wings and a rubber ring to go around
her waist.

Millie and Aunt Pearl paddled out into the waves until
the water came up to the top of Millie's legs.   Then they
were not quite sure what to do next.

"Push out with your arms," said one little boy who was
swimming nearby.

"Kick out with your legs," said a girl as she splashed
along like a small frog.

But Millie felt rather nervous.

Then she saw something silvery in the water. Perhaps it
was a mermaid! She pushed her hands through the water,
trying to catch the sparkling tail.

Millie liked the feeling of the water flowing over her arms.
"I'll try the feet bit tomorrow," she promised Aunt Pearl.

The next day Millie didn't quite dare to take her feet off the bottom. But suddenly she glimpsed a fish-shaped tail glinting by the rocks. It must be the mermaid again! Millie wanted to see her so much! Bravely she took first one foot and then the other off the bottom.

She moved her arms and kicked her legs together.
 "That's marvellous, Millie," exclaimed Aunt Pearl.
"You are doing well."

Each day Millie grew more confident. Little by little
Aunt Pearl let out the air from her water-wings.
    And, finally, one day Millie was swimming all by
herself! It still felt as if something was holding her
up but it wasn't the water-wings or the rubber ring.

Suddenly, out of the corner of her eye, Millie saw the flash of a silver tail in the waves beneath her. It *must* be the mermaid.

"Look, Aunt Pearl," cried Millie. "The mermaid is helping me to swim!"

"I can't see anyone," said Aunt Pearl. "You're swimming all by yourself, Millie."

"Why don't you come in too, Auntie," she said.
"Swimming is easy!"
    "Hang on a minute!" called Aunt Pearl.

In a few minutes she was ready, wearing a big pair of water-wings just like Millie's.

"Well, dear," she said, jumping into the water, "perhaps now we can both be mermaids!"